W0114245

She
Persisted

··

NAOMI OSAKA

··

— INSPIRED BY —

She Persisted

by Chelsea Clinton & Alexandra Boiger

. . . .

NAOMI OSAKA

. . . .

written by
Kekla Magoon

interior illustrations by
Gillian Flint

PHILOMEL

PHILOMEL
An imprint of Penguin Random House LLC, New York

First published in the United States of America by Philomel,
an imprint of Penguin Random House LLC, 2024

Text copyright © 2024 by Chelsea Clinton
Illustrations copyright © 2024 by Alexandra Boiger

Penguin supports copyright. Copyright fuels creativity, encourages diverse voices, promotes
free speech, and creates a vibrant culture. Thank you for buying an authorized edition of this
book and for complying with copyright laws by not reproducing, scanning, or distributing any
part of it in any form without permission. You are supporting writers and allowing Penguin
to continue to publish books for every reader.

Philomel is a registered trademark of Penguin Random House LLC.
The Penguin colophon is a registered trademark of Penguin Books Limited.

Visit us online at PenguinRandomHouse.com.

Library of Congress Cataloging-in-Publication Data is available.

ISBN 9780593623534 (hardcover)
ISBN 9780593623541 (paperback)

2nd Printing

Printed in the United States of America

LSCC

Edited by Talia Benamy.
Design by Ellice M. Lee.
Text set in LTC Kennerley Pro.

The publisher does not have any control over and does not assume any responsibility for
author or third-party websites or their content.

For

Ginger—tennis fan and tireless champion

DEAR READER,

As Sally Ride and Marian Wright Edelman both powerfully said, "You can't be what you can't see." When Sally said that, she meant that it was hard to dream of being an astronaut, like she was, or a doctor or an athlete or anything at all if you didn't see someone like you who already had lived that dream. She especially was talking about seeing women in jobs that historically were held by men.

I wrote the first *She Persisted* and the books that came after it because I wanted young girls—and children of all genders—to see women who worked hard to live their dreams. And I wanted all of us to see examples of persistence in the face of different challenges to help inspire us in our own lives.

I'm so thrilled now to partner with a sisterhood of writers to bring longer, more in-depth versions of these stories of women's persistence and achievement to readers. I hope you enjoy these chapter books as much as I do and find them inspiring and empowering.

And remember: If anyone ever tells you no, if anyone ever says your voice isn't important or your dreams are too big, remember these women. They persisted and so should you.

Warmly,
Chelsea Clinton

She
Persisted

She Persisted: DEB HAALAND

She Persisted: BETHANY HAMILTON

She Persisted: DOROTHY HEIGHT

She Persisted: DOLORES HUERTA

She Persisted: FLORENCE GRIFFITH JOYNER

She Persisted: HELEN KELLER

She Persisted: CORETTA SCOTT KING

She Persisted: OPAL LEE

She Persisted: CLARA LEMLICH

She Persisted: RACHEL LEVINE

She Persisted: MAYA LIN

She Persisted: WANGARI MAATHAI

NAOMI OSAKA

TABLE OF CONTENTS

....

....

Taking to the Court

Naomi Osaka was born in Japan on October 16, 1997, a child of two very different worlds. Her mother, Tamaki Osaka, is Japanese. Her father, Leonard Francois, is a Black man from Haiti. Being biracial and multicultural has always been an important part of Naomi's life. Most of the time, it makes her feel happy and special— it is exciting to have several cultures to claim. It is powerful to hear about how her mother's childhood and her father's childhood were different, and to compare their stories to her own. It is wonderful to be able to speak and understand multiple languages: English, Japanese, and even some Haitian Creole. But being biracial comes with some challenges, too.

In many places all around the world, including the United States, people have been slow to accept interracial couples and their children. Japan is one of those places, too. Living in Japan as a biracial couple was often challenging for Tamaki and Leonard. Even Tamaki's family didn't approve of their marriage at first. It made Tamaki sad that they couldn't spend time with her parents, but she loved Leonard and wanted to build a new family with him.

Tamaki and Leonard wanted their biracial

children to fit into Japanese culture as well as possible, and having a Japanese last name could help.
So Naomi and her older sister, Mari, were both
given their mother's last name. Still, many people

were not accepting of their family. Strangers often stared at them in public. Sometimes people said unkind things to Naomi and her sister. Their comments were hurtful.

The family of four moved from Japan to the United States when Naomi was three years old. They lived in New York State, on Long Island, with Leonard's family. Naomi and Mari got to know all about Haitian culture, enjoying spicy food, energetic music, and family connections. At home, their mother spoke Japanese to them and cooked Japanese food, too, and so they felt like they were part of both cultures.

Naomi and Mari began playing tennis with their dad. Every day, they spent time on the public courts near their home, hitting hundreds of balls back and forth. Leonard was fascinated by the rise of two Black teenage tennis stars, Venus and Serena Williams. The Williams sisters had both become world-class tennis players, all because their father encouraged and trained them from a very young age. Leonard wondered if something similar could be possible for his own daughters.

Naomi had mixed feelings about all that effort. "I'm happy he made us do it now," she later said, looking back on the hundreds of hours they spent practicing when she was a child. But at the time, she felt jealous of other kids who got to go on summer vacations and have fun while she was practicing endlessly.

Naomi's family moved to Florida when she was eight years old so that she and Mari could train year-round. They practiced on the court for eight hours each day. The girls were homeschooled

at night. It took a lot of dedication to show up day after day, but Naomi and Mari showed promise at the sport, so their parents pushed them hard, and the girls rose to the challenge.

Life in the United States was going well, but Naomi's mother wanted the girls to finally connect with her side of the family. When Naomi was eleven, they visited Japan to meet her grandparents and other relatives. The girls spoke Japanese well enough to interact, but their extended family struggled to understand their tennis practice and homeschooling lifestyle. It seemed strange to others for Naomi and Mari to be chasing the unlikely dream of being tennis stars. "So many people have told my dad that I would never be anything," Naomi said. But the girls kept pursuing their goal.

Even Naomi sometimes wondered if all the effort was worth it. She often longed to go to school with other children, something she saw as more "normal" than the life she was living. "No one really knows all the sacrifices that you make just to be good," Naomi said. But in the long run, those sacrifices would lead her to success.

CHAPTER 2

Defining Success

When it came time to compete at tennis, Naomi had to make a big choice: Which country would she represent? The United States, where she had grown up and still lived? Haiti, where her father was from and where she felt cul-turally connected? Japan, where she was born?

In her heart, Naomi knew all of these places were part of her identity. She once said, "As long as I can remember, people have struggled to define me. I've never really fit into one description—but people are so fast to give me a label. *Is she Japanese? American? Haitian? Black? Asian?* Well, I'm all of these things together at the same time." But the rules of the International Tennis Federation (ITF) required her to choose one country. Even though she had grown up in the United States, Naomi said, "I don't necessarily feel like I'm American." So Naomi and her parents decided she would compete for Japan.

Naomi began competing in ITF matches as soon as she was old enough. She played her first professional match on her fourteenth birthday: October 16, 2011. It was the first of many matches to come.

As a new player, Naomi needed to play in at least eighteen tournaments each year and win as many matches as possible to earn a place in the international player rankings. Tennis tournaments are played elimination-style. Many players enter and are paired up to play individual matches. The winners move on to play other winners, and the losers are out of the tournament. This continues until only one champion remains unbeaten. Usually, there are a total of 128 players in the "main draw" of a tournament. This even number breaks down to eight groups of sixteen players who compete in the first four elimination rounds, leading to eight players who compete in the quarterfinals, four in the semifinals, and two in the final match.

Naomi played in more and more tournaments, and her results in each tournament earned her points that gave her an international ranking.

She was on the charts! But there are typically more than a thousand ranked female tennis players each year. The best tournament options are open to players in the top five hundred. Those in the top one hundred receive the most sponsorship money, which helps support them as they play. After her first full year of tournaments, at the end of 2012, Naomi was ranked number 1,019. It would be a long climb to get to the top one hundred. But Naomi was determined to make it.

Professional tennis players also get paid based on their performance in each tournament. It is very expensive to train as a tennis player, and the prize money helps players keep training to compete. Players who win a lot can afford good quality equipment. They can hire the most experienced coaches. Every tennis player dreams of winning a major tournament—partly for the big ranking boost and partly for the prize money.

The four biggest tennis tournaments each year are called Grand Slams. They include the Australian Open, the French Open, Wimbledon (held in England), and the US Open. The term "open" means that any ranked player can try to qualify. But even so, 104 places are reserved in the tournament for the top-ranked players to automatically enter. That leaves twenty-four spots available for others to compete. Sixteen of those spots are given to players who win three qualifying matches. The last eight spots are reserved for "wild cards," players who get a special invitation to participate.

All tennis tournaments pay the winners, but Grand Slam prize money is huge. In 2012,

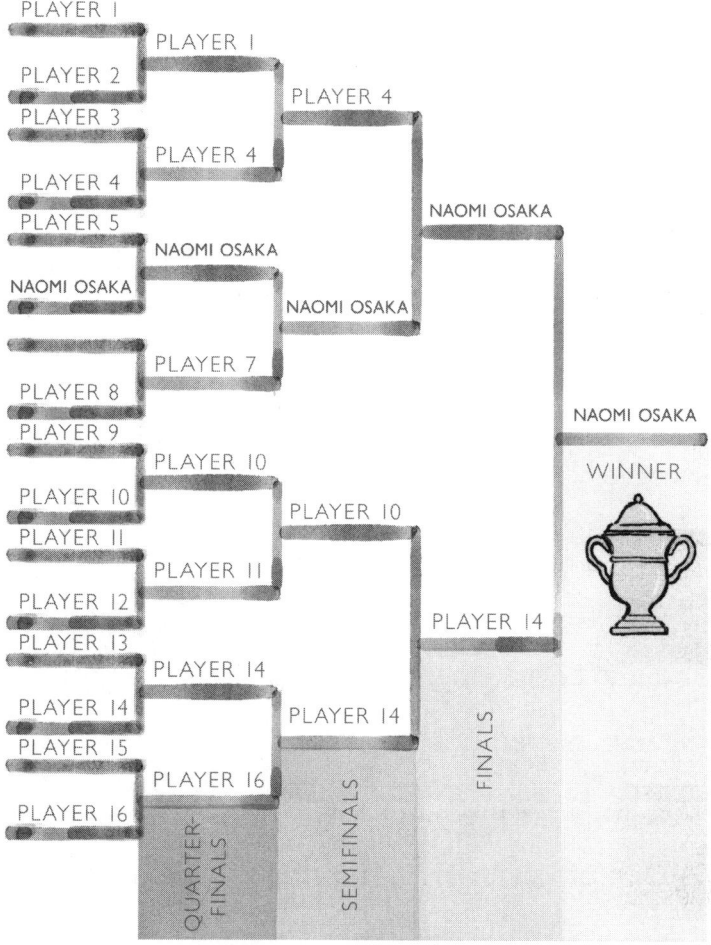

the women's winner at the US Open received
$1.9 million. Even the players who lose in early
rounds can make tens of thousands of dollars. In

2012, first-round players received $23,000. That much money could buy a lot of practice balls and rackets! But that first year, Naomi didn't come anywhere close to qualifying for the US Open. She still had a long way to go to meet her goals. And she knew she would have to work hard to make it.

Naomi competed in smaller tournaments for several years as she worked to rise in the rankings. She played in singles matches on her own, and she also played doubles matches with Mari. She won a lot of games, but she lost a lot too. She had to keep practicing and growing as a player. It was difficult and sometimes frustrating, but Naomi felt determined to solve the problems in front of her. "You have to be really mentally strong to play tennis," Naomi said. "You just have to keep going out there every day trying to figure stuff out and just keep adjusting."

It was challenging, but Naomi persisted, even when the going got tough. She and her family constantly worked and changed their routines and adapted, in search of the best training model for Naomi. Her parents had been her coaches most of her life, but professional players need professional coaches, too. Naomi tried a few elite tennis training academies, looking for the right fit. She studied with Patrick Tauma at ISP Academy, then moved to Harold Solomon Tennis Academy, and later to ProWorld Tennis Academy.

All the while, Naomi kept attending tournaments and playing qualifying matches, hoping to finally earn a spot in the main draw. But it was very difficult to win three matches in a row.

The first time Naomi achieved the main draw in a tournament, it was in doubles with Mari. But she played (and lost) qualifying matches in several singles tournaments before she broke into the main draw in one. When she made her first main draw on her own, it was an exciting day! Naomi knew she was finally making progress. Even though she had not yet won a tournament, Naomi didn't give up—she knew she had to keep trying and keep improving. And that was just what she was going to do.

···

Championship Mindset

Finally, in June 2013, while Naomi was playing at a tournament in Texas, she made it all the way to the finals. It was her first time doing that! She had been playing professionally for a year and a half at that point. Nine months later, in March 2014, she made it to her second-ever finals, this time in Mexico. She did not win either match, but she continued improving her game and setting her sights higher. She was on the rise!

Naomi joined the Women's Tennis Association Tour in 2014, when she made the main draw in the Bank of the West Classic in Stanford. She was sixteen years old and ranked number 406 in the world. She was paired in a first-round match against Samantha Stosur, who was ranked number 19. Naomi knew it would be good experience to play such a highly ranked woman. Nobody thought she had a chance of winning . . . but she did! The surprising upset kept her in the tournament longer than expected, and by the end of the season, she was near the top 250.

In 2015, Naomi qualified for her first two Grand Slams—Wimbledon and the US Open—but she didn't make the main draw in either. In 2016, she neared the top 100 and made her first Grand Slam main draw at the Australian Open. At the

Miami Open that year, Naomi won a match in an upset against yet another higher-ranked player and finally broke into the top 100. She reached the third round at the US Open and competed so well all year that the Women's Tennis Association (WTA) named her the Newcomer of the Year.

The following year was rough. Naomi attended a lot of tournaments, but she didn't win very much. With disappointment building, she knew she had to improve to keep moving forward, so she hired a new coach, Sascha Bajin. He had worked with one of Naomi's role models, Serena Williams. It seemed like a great fit at first. The year 2018 dawned strongly for Naomi. She practiced long and hard, and she steadily rose in the WTA rankings.

Naomi won her first tournament in Indian

Wells, California, that spring. Soon after that, she achieved one of her lifelong goals: facing Serena Williams on the court. Naomi played against Serena in the third round of the Miami Open, and she won!

Amazingly, she faced Serena a second time that year when she made it to the 2018 US Open final. It was Naomi's first time getting to the finals at a Grand Slam tournament, and she was playing against her biggest idol. She had never faced a more pressure-filled game in her career. But Naomi rose to the occasion.

Even when an argument erupted between Serena and the umpire in the middle of the match, Naomi kept her cool. She tried to block out the noise and play her best. She defeated Serena in the final and became US Open champion. She was the first Japanese player to ever win a Grand Slam—an amazing achievement!

Many media outlets called Naomi an "overnight sensation." Journalists wrote articles about her that made it sound like she had come from nowhere to defeat a champion. But Naomi knew that her victory had happened because she had worked hard for many years to reach success. She had a long record of wins and losses alike over many hard-fought matches, not to mention countless hours of practice behind her.

Naomi followed up her US Open victory by winning the Australian Open at the start of the next season. She became the first tennis player in over twenty years to win their first two Grand Slam finals, and the first woman to win back-to-back Grand Slam tournaments in a decade. After

that victory, Naomi was ranked number one in the world!

But then things got a bit rocky for her. Naomi parted ways with her new coach after barely a year together. Many people were surprised by her decision. She had been playing very well under Coach Bajin, but Naomi told reporters, "My reason is I wouldn't put success over my happiness—that's my main thing. I'm not going to sacrifice that."

Naomi didn't give the public very many details about what she meant when she said that, but she admitted there had been tension between her and her coach during the Australian Open. She had followed her instincts in separating from him. She took on a temporary new coach, Jermaine Jenkins, and then for a while

she returned to being coached by her dad.

Everything that was going on behind the scenes affected Naomi's performance on the court. Throughout 2019, she struggled with injuries that forced her to withdraw or retire early from several tournaments. As the losses piled up and her place in the rankings dropped, Naomi worried that she hadn't fully adopted a championship mindset yet, but she persisted through the difficulties and kept showing up to matches over and over again, doing her best. She was still determined to reclaim her top ranking and become a champion once again.

....

CHAPTER 4

Say Their Names

At the beginning of 2020, Naomi was going strong and playing hard. She had hired a new coach, Wim Fissette, and even with her more recent challenges, the glow of her two Grand Slam championships was still strong. She had a massive fan base in both the United States and Japan—in fact, Naomi's biracial, multicultural identity and her international experience were helping her win over Japanese fans. Naomi was showing the world that you didn't have to look exactly one way in order to be Japanese.

Naomi went to the Australian Open in January looking to defend her title. She was disappointed when she lost to Coco Gauff in the third round, but she immediately started working on improving her game for the rest of the season. Off the court, Naomi used her new celebrity status to support other interests. She developed a fashion line with a Japanese American designer, ADEAM, and debuted it at New York Fashion Week in February.

Then something sad and scary happened. People in Asia began getting very sick from a terrible disease caused by a virus. The symptoms were similar to the common cold at first, but in many cases people got so sick, they had to go to

the hospital. Soon, the virus spread out of Asia, and people in Europe and North America began getting sick too. The virus spread to people in Africa and South America and Australia, becoming a global pandemic, which meant everyone in the whole world was at risk of getting sick and possibly dying. Hundreds, then thousands, then millions of people did die from the illness, which was called COVID-19.

Major cities around the world shut down, and people stayed home to stop the spread of the virus. People began wearing face masks to protect themselves and each other, because the virus could spread through the air when people coughed, sneezed, or breathed. Flights were canceled to prevent sick travelers from bringing the virus to new areas. The virus could spread most easily in large gatherings of people, so events that drew big crowds—like tennis tournaments—got canceled too. Soon, the prospects of playing any tennis at all looked rather dim. The world was in crisis, and that took priority.

The COVID-19 pandemic and global shutdown was a worldwide tragedy, and it was also a huge setback for Naomi. She returned home to Los Angeles, where she now lived. She paid attention to the news and hoped to hear that the pandemic was ending. But that news didn't come. More and more tennis tournaments were canceled—the entire tour shut down from March through July of 2020. Many people were still getting sick and dying.

One night in May, Naomi saw reports of a tragedy that had happened in Minneapolis, Minnesota. A police officer named Derek Chauvin had killed a man named George Floyd on the street outside of a grocery store. A witness recorded a cell phone video of Officer Chauvin's actions. The video showed that what could have been a simple arrest had somehow turned into a violent and cruel murder.

The news about George Floyd's death was very upsetting. People in Minneapolis took to the streets, marching and protesting this act of police brutality. The term "police brutality" refers to moments when police officers use too much force in dealing with people. In the United States, police brutality is sometimes linked to racial bias. George Floyd was Black and Officer Chauvin was white, and racism was almost certainly part of what led Officer Chauvin to murder George Floyd.

The thousands of protestors who marched that night demanded justice for George Floyd and for all victims of police brutality. There had been hundreds of unarmed Black people across the country killed by police officers over the years, and very few police officers were held accountable, even when it was clear that too much force had been used. The protestors wanted to make sure that Officer Chauvin would be held accountable for his actions.

Watching the protests on television, Naomi felt a strong urge to do something to help. As a Black person with celebrity status, she wondered if she could use her voice to advocate for justice for George Floyd and others like him.

Naomi and her boyfriend, Cordae, traveled to Minnesota to support the protests. There, she witnessed the grief of Black people as they mourned George Floyd. They also grieved over the state of the policing system. Many felt powerless to change it. Taking to the streets was the best way they could think of to try to be heard.

"Being on the ground in Minneapolis was what felt right at that moment," Naomi said. "I kept asking myself what can I do [and] I decided it was time to speak up about systemic racism and police brutality."

Naomi was not alone. Athletes across sports felt the same way. Many players and even entire teams wore BLACK LIVES MATTER on their jerseys to support a movement for racial justice. Others took a knee during the national anthem or refused to play in protest of police brutality and systemic racism across American culture.

Naomi took a stand with her protest at the Cincinnati Open in August 2020. It was the first big tournament to come back since the pandemic began. But Naomi refused to play. She announced her intent to withdraw from the tournament in solidarity with the Black Lives Matter protests. Surprisingly, instead of causing her to forfeit, the

Cincinnati Open organizers chose to support her protest. They shut down the entire tournament for the day. No one played. "She stopped the game of tennis for a day, which had never been done in history," said her coach.

"It was a bit frightening to speak up," Naomi said, but she knew it was important. She created special face masks to wear at her next tournament, the US Open. Each mask had the name of an unarmed Black person who had been killed, including George Floyd. She brought seven masks—one for each round of the Open— but she would only get to wear them all if she made it to the final. The other names she chose were: Breonna Taylor, Elijah McClain, Ahmaud Arbery, Trayvon Martin, Philando Castile, and Tamir Rice.

"It's quite sad that seven masks isn't enough for the amount of names," she said. Naomi knew that many more than seven people had been killed in similar tragic ways. But she also knew that she had to do something, even if it didn't feel like enough. "The platform that I have right now . . . I feel like I should be using it for something."

Naomi drew strength from using her status to voice support for fellow Black Americans. Her hopes came true—she got to wear the last of her seven masks when she made it to the US Open final.

And then she won.

....

CHAPTER 5

Priorities

Naomi was named *Sports Illustrated* Sportsperson of the Year at the end of 2020, due to her combination of activism and athleticism. She won the Australian Open in January 2021, making it the second time she had won two Grand Slams back-to-back. But behind the scenes, she was struggling. Naomi's competitive drive wasn't the only thing going on inside her mind— she was affected by anxiety and depression too.

Anxiety made her worry a lot, and depression made her feel very sad sometimes for no specific reason. She took medicine to help her feel better, but it was still a challenge.

Naomi realized that part of her anxiety was coming from the sudden spotlight. Ever since she had become a Grand Slam champion, the media had been paying close attention to her. She had millions of fans, a public image to maintain, and a fashion brand to define and promote. It was a lot of pressure. "The amount of attention that I get is kind of ridiculous," she said. "No one prepares you for that."

Naomi needed a break from the spotlight. She knew she could perform better on the court if she didn't have to do interviews before and after every match. She needed to focus on her game.

The problem was, some tournaments required the players to spend a certain amount of time face-to-face with the press.

At the 2021 French Open, Naomi took a stand. She wrote to the organizers and explained her concerns. Then she announced to her social media followers that she would not be doing press at the tournament.

The organizers did not accept Naomi's explanation. They fined her $15,000 for refusing to do the required interviews. She protested the requirement, saying that sometimes facing the press takes too big a toll on her mindset. "People have no regard for athletes' mental health," she said. "We're often . . . asked questions that bring doubt into our minds, and I'm just not going to subject myself to people that doubt me."

But the French Open organizers declared that they would continue to fine her more and more if she didn't do interviews after each round of play. They threatened to expel her from the tournament entirely. So Naomi decided to withdraw on her own.

Naomi clearly made the right choice to take care of herself, but her actions stirred up conversation and controversy around the world. Many people applauded her for taking a stand. Some even criticized the French Open and argued that the rules should be changed. But other people called her weak. Athletes like Naomi make a lot of money, they argued, and speaking to fans through the press is part of their job.

Naomi's stance caused many people to reconsider the demands placed upon athletes. Some other tennis players and even athletes from different sports began telling the press they agreed with Naomi. There were still a lot of naysayers, but Naomi persisted in doing what was most important—taking care of herself. She pulled out of other tournaments that spring to focus on her health and personal life.

Naomi still had many fans and supporters around the world. She was seen as such an important representative of Japan that she got chosen for a special opportunity: lighting the Olympic cauldron at the 2020 Olympics in Tokyo. This took place in the summer of 2021, because the Games had been postponed for a year due to the pandemic. The Olympic flame had been brought all the way from Greece on torches carried by a series of athletes from around the world. To be the very last torch bearer is a position of honor. When the final runner arrived in the stadium, the crowd of over ten thousand people waited to see who it would be . . . then Naomi Osaka jogged in. A roaring cheer went up from the crowd. Naomi carried the torch toward the cauldron and lit it, officially opening the Games.

Naomi made it to the third round in the Olympics, which was a rather disappointing result for her. Later, she wished she had handled her Olympic experience differently, and she wasn't just talking about her loss. She said the cauldron-lighting moment was "fire," or incredibly exciting, and that she should have stopped to enjoy each glorious moment after that even more. "That's gonna be really important in

my life going forward," she told her Instagram followers. "Just enjoying the experiences and making the most out of the time."

Naomi was determined to live her best life.

....

A Book, a Baby, and Balance

The following year, 2022, was another low year in terms of tennis winnings, but Naomi was feeling happier with her life overall. She worked hard to balance her mental health with her ambition to train hard, play hard, and win matches.

Naomi received many sponsorships from companies in the United States and Japan. These companies paid her to appear in ads. She also used their products and told her fans about them. Naomi continued developing her fashion brand, even partnering with Victoria's Secret (a famous underwear company) to create her own line. She continued her advocacy and activism about mental health and racial justice.

In 2022, Naomi released a picture book called *The Way Champs Play*. It is a story about how anyone can play like a champion if they are determined to practice, work hard, and have fun.

Naomi was scheduled to play in the 2023 Australian Open, but shortly before the tournament she withdrew. It was for an exciting reason—Naomi was pregnant! She and Cordae were expecting a baby that summer, so Naomi announced that she would take the 2023 season

off. She still practiced and worked to stay in shape to return to the court in 2024.

Naomi had her baby in July 2023. She felt as strongly as ever that she wanted to continue to become the best version of herself so that she could be the best possible mother to her daughter. "I'm taking it day by day and just trying to be someone that my . . . daughter will be proud of," she said.

When Naomi returns from maternity leave, she will likely be able to retain her Top-100 WTA ranking, even if she has not played any matches in over a year. This is a recent development in the history of the Women's Tennis Association— it used to be that pregnant athletes would lose their ranking during their time away. Many jobs offer maternity leave options. In fact, US law requires most employers to allow a pregnant person to take time off and return. But tennis is a different kind of job. When Naomi's role model, Serena Williams, took time off to have a baby in

2017, the WTA offered no option for maternity leave. When she came back to tennis, Serena had to start from scratch and play her way back to the top of the rankings. The WTA changed their rules in 2018 to make it easier for leading players to have children and still return to work.

Naomi is someone who wants to win, but not at the expense of her happiness, her personal life, and her voice. She said, "As high-level athletes, we are accustomed to being trained to win at all costs, but actually there are more important things in life, and it doesn't define who we are as people." This is an important lesson that she learned over the years, and that she tries hard to share with others. Still, her legacy and impact on the sport of tennis are already permanent and powerful.

"I love the thought of a biracial girl in a class-room in Japan glowing with pride when I win a Grand Slam," Naomi said. "I really hope that the playground is a friendlier place for her now that she can point to a role model and be proud of who she is. And dream big."

In her career, in her activism, and in so many other areas of life, Naomi Osaka showed the world that working hard and sticking to what you believe can make a difference. She persisted, and you can too!

HOW YOU CAN PERSIST

By Kekla Magoon

Naomi Osaka is a strong role model for all of us. By following her example, anyone can persist and grow stronger. Naomi teaches us how to stay focused on a goal, explore our many gifts, care for our mental health, and raise our voices to support the causes we care about. Here are some ways that you can follow in her footsteps!

1. Do you have a favorite sport or activity? Practice it as often as you can to improve your skills.

2. If you have several favorite activities, practice them all! Naomi is a champion in tennis, but she also enjoys fashion, so she has made that part of her brand too. Make a list of hobbies you enjoy that could be a bigger part of your life.

3. Research a few recent champions in your favorite sport. What did they achieve? What challenges did they overcome? What can you learn from their example?

4. Think about your goals. What will it take to achieve them? Make plans and talk about them with people you care about.

5. Naomi was never alone in persisting. Her family, friends, competitors, and

coaches encouraged her every step of the way. How can you support and encourage the people you care about?

6. Naomi prioritizes her mental health by being honest about her feelings. When she is upset, or scared, or feeling down, she lets the people around her know so that they can support her even more. Take a moment to check in with yourself at least once every day—how do you feel?

7. If you ever encounter a moment when you feel extremely sad or life feels very overwhelming, you are not alone. Many people have these feelings every day. Reach out to an adult you trust and let them know so that they can

help. If it's too hard to talk to someone you know, there are helpful adults you can speak to at the National Suicide Prevention Lifeline. Just dial 988 to speak with one of them.

8. Speak up about issues you care about. What is important to you? How can you use your voice to create awareness, like Naomi does?

9. Naomi uses her voice to advocate for racial justice. How can you be an advocate for racial justice in your own school or community? Researching local organizations that work for equality in your hometown is one place to start.

Acknowledgments

I love playing and watching tennis! I've even been to the US Open to see athletes like Serena Williams compete for the title live, and I'm grateful for that exciting experience. Someday, maybe I'll be lucky enough to see Naomi herself play. She's such an inspiration!

Thank you to editors Talia Benamy and Jill Santopolo, along with the whole team at Philomel, for trusting me with Naomi's story—it's a pleasure to write about her. I'm grateful to Chelsea Clinton for having the vision for this series and for inviting me to join the Persisterhood. My agent, Ginger Knowlton, and my own supportive team of friends and family help me succeed every day. Especially, thanks to Naomi Osaka for being an exceptional role model for all of us. She is truly a champion!

❧ References ❧

Ackerman, McCarton. "Is Naomi Osaka Ready for a Grand Slam Title?" USOpen.org, September 3, 2018. usopen.org/en_US/news/articles/2018-09-03/is_naomi_osaka_ready_for_a_grand_slam_title.html.

Bradley, Garrett, director. *Naomi Osaka.* Netflix, 2021. netflix.com/title/81128594.

Etienne, Vanessa. "Naomi Osaka Says Athletes Are Taught to 'Win at All Costs' at Expense

of 'More Important Things.'" *People*, June 1,
2022. people.com/sports/naomi-osaka-says
-athletes-are-taught-to-win-at-all-costs-dazed
-cover.

Hislop, Madeline. "Naomi Osaka Opens Up
About Depression and Anxiety as She
Withdraws from French Open." Women's
Agenda, May 31, 2021. womensagenda.com
.au/latest/naomi-osaka-opens-up-about
-depression-and-anxiety-as-she-withdraws
-from-french-open.

Igoe, Katherine J. "Naomi Osaka's Parents,
Leonard Francois and Tamaki Osaka, Are
Her Biggest Fans." *Marie Claire*, June 1, 2021.
marieclaire.com/celebrity/a33979330/naomi
-osaka-parents.

Kimble, Lindsay. "Naomi Osaka Withdraws from

French Open after Skipping Press, Says She Deals with Depression." *People*, May 31, 2021. people.com/sports/naomi-osaka-withdraws -from-french-open-2021-mental-health.

Larmer, Brook. "Naomi Osaka's Breakthrough Game." *New York Times Magazine*, August 23, 2018. nytimes.com/2018/08/23/magazine /naomi-osakas-breakthrough-game.html.

Latimer, Jolene. "Who Is Naomi Osaka's Boyfriend? All About Cordae." *People*, January 11, 2023, updated June 6, 2023. people.com/sports/who-is-cordae-naomi -osaka.

Martin, Jill. "Following Serena Williams' Return, WTA Changes Rules on Ranking after Pregnancy and Dress Code." CNN.com,

December 21, 2018. cnn.com/2018/12/18
/tennis/wta-rule-changes-ranking-after
-pregnancy-dress-code-trnd/index.html.

Martin, Jill. "Naomi Osaka Says She Won't
Do Press Conferences during the French
Open." CNN.com, May 27, 2021. edition
.cnn.com/2021/05/26/tennis/naomi-osaka
-no-press-conferences-at-french-open-spt-intl
/index.html.

Mitchell, Kevin. "Naomi Osaka's Split with
Sascha Bejin a Sign of the Times and Her
Steeliness." *The Guardian*, February 12, 2019.
theguardian.com/sport/2019/feb/12/naomi
-osaka-sascha-bajin-tennis-kevin-mitchell.

"Naomi Osaka: Split with Coach Was Refusal to
Put 'Success over Happiness.'" *The Guardian*,

February 18, 2019. theguardian.com/sport
/2019/feb/18/naomi-osaka-coach-split
-happiness-dubai-wta-tennis.

"Naomi Osaka Talks New Children's Book,
'The Way Champs Play.'" *Good Morning
America*. YouTube, December 6, 2022.
youtube.com/watch?v=pXS9YGSxZ_c.

Osaka, Naomi. "I Never Would've Imagined
Writing This Two Years Ago." *Esquire*,
July 1, 2020. esquire.com/sports/a33022329
/naomi-osaka-op-ed-george-floyd-protests.

Osaka, Naomi. "Naomi Osaka: 'It's O.K. Not
to Be O.K.'" *Time*, July 8, 2021. time.com
/6077128/naomi-osaka-essay-tokyo-olympics
/?utm_source=roundup&campaign=olympics.

"Superstar Tennis Champ Naomi Osaka on
the Joys of Going Unrecognized in Public."

The Late Show with Stephen Colbert.
YouTube, December 6, 2022. youtube.com
/watch?v=2WeLksKrb4k.

Williams, Madison. "Naomi Osaka Says She
'Regrets' Experience at Tokyo Olympics Via
Instagram Post." *Sports Illustrated*, February
19, 2022. si.com/extra-mustard/2022/02/19
/naomi-osaka-regrets-tokyo-olympics-instagram.

KEKLA MAGOON writes novels and non-fiction for young readers, including *The Highest Tribute: Thurgood Marshall's Life, Leadership, and Legacy*, *Today the World Is Watching You: The Little Rock Nine and the Fight for School Integration 1957*, *The Season of Styx Malone*, and *The Rock and the River*. She has received the *Boston Globe-Horn Book* Award, an NAACP Image Award, the John Steptoe New Talent Award, and four Coretta Scott King Honors, and been long listed for the National Book Award. Kekla conducts school and library visits nationwide. She holds a BA from Northwestern University and an MFA in writing from Vermont College of Fine Arts, where she now serves on faculty.

Photo credit: Alice Dodge

You can visit Kekla Magoon online at
KeklaMagoon.com
or follow her on Instagram
@keklamagoon

GILLIAN FLINT has worked as a professional illustrator since earning an animation and illustration degree in 2003. Her work has since been published in the UK, USA and Australia. In her spare time, Gillian enjoys reading, spending time with her family and pottering about in the garden on sunny days. She lives in the northwest of England.

Courtesy of the illustrator

You can visit Gillian Flint online at
GillianFlint.com
and on Instagram
@gillianflint_illustration

CHELSEA CLINTON is the author of the #1 *New York Times* bestseller *She Persisted: 13 American Women Who Changed the World*; *She Persisted Around the World: 13 Women Who Changed History*; *She Persisted in Sports: American Olympians Who Changed the Game*; *She Persisted in Science: Brilliant Women Who Made a Difference*; *Don't Let Them Disappear: 12 Endangered Species Across the Globe*; *Welcome to the Big Kids Club*; *It's Your World: Get Informed, Get Inspired & Get Going!*; *Start Now!: You Can Make a Difference*; with Hillary Clinton, *Grandma's Gardens* and *Gutsy Women*; and, with Devi Sridhar, *Governing Global Health: Who Runs the World and Why?* She is also the Vice Chair of the Clinton Foundation, where she works on many initiatives, including those that help empower the next generation of leaders. She lives in New York City with her husband, Marc, and their children.

Courtesy of the author

You can follow Chelsea Clinton on Twitter
@ChelseaClinton
or on Facebook at
facebook.com/chelseaclinton

ALEXANDRA BOIGER has illustrated nearly twenty picture books, including *the She Persisted books* by Chelsea Clinton; the popular Tallulah series by Marilyn Singer; and the Max and Marla books, which she also wrote. Originally from Munich, Germany, she now lives outside of San Francisco, California, with her husband, Andrea, daughter, Vanessa, and two cats, Luiso and Winter.

Photo credit: *Vanessa Blasich*

You can visit Alexandra Boiger online at
AlexandraBoiger.com
or follow her on Instagram
@alexandra_boiger

Read about more inspiring women in the

She Persisted series!